HELP!
I'M TRAPPED
IN SANTA'S BODY

Other Books By Todd Strasser

HELP!
I'M TRAPPED
IN SANTA'S BODY

TODD STRASSER

AN
APPLE
PAPERBACK

SCHOLASTIC INC.
New York Toronto London Auckland Sydney

ISBN 0-590-02972-X

Text copyright © 1997 by Todd Strasser. All rights reserved. Published by Scholastic Inc. APPLE PAPERBACKS and logos are trademarks and/or registered trademarks of Scholastic Inc.

12 11 10 9 8 7 6 5 4 3 2 1   7 8 9/9 0 1 2/0

Printed in the U.S.A.

First Scholastic printing, November 1997

To Joanna Cole, whom I adore

1

"The best thing would be if you got to be Santa himself," I said. "Then you could give yourself every Christmas present you wanted."

"I wouldn't want to be Santa," said Josh.

"Why not?" asked our friend Andy.

It was a Saturday afternoon three weeks before Christmas. My friends and I had nothing to do, so we were sitting in my kitchen making up our Christmas lists.

"Have you ever seen a picture of that guy?" Josh asked. "If you were Santa then you'd have his butt. And that's one mighty big butt."

"I wouldn't talk about Santa like that if I were you," Andy warned him.

"Why not?" Josh asked.

"Because he might hear you," Andy said.

"Give me a break," Josh scoffed. "Santa Claus doesn't exist." He cupped his hands around his mouth and yelled up at the ceiling, *Hey! Santa Butt! Can you hear me?*"

Andy winced. "If you're wrong about him, you're gonna be in big trouble."

Ha-choo! I sneezed, then blew my nose. I was just getting over a cold.

"I wouldn't mind having Santa's butt," I said. "It's his beard I wouldn't want."

"What's wrong with his beard?" Andy asked.

"Well, it's the mustache, really," I said. "I mean, when Santa blows his nose, that mustache must get all full of boogers and stuff."

"You're right, Jake," Josh agreed. "I bet you can see those big green Christmas boogers a mile away in that white mustache."

"You better hope he's not listening," Andy cautioned.

Josh smirked and cupped his hands around his mouth again. *"Yo, Santa Butt! Are you listening? I said big green Christmas boogers!"*

Andy shook his head and sighed as if he thought that some day Josh would regret saying that. I picked up a piece of paper with my Christmas list on it.

"Okay, guys," I said. "Here's what I've decided I want: the Turbo game system, the snowboard, and the Bubonic Plague CD."

"I'm getting the game system, the snowboard, the CD, *and* the Sky Walk basketball shoes," said Andy.

"Then I'm getting the game system, snowboard, CD, basketball shoes, *and* the Fat Wheels mountain bike," Josh said.

"Forget about the Fat Wheels mountain bike," I said. "They had it on the news last night. It's the hottest item this Christmas. You can't find them *anywhere*. And if you did, they'd probably charge you a fortune for one."

"If I asked Santa, I bet he could get me one," Andy said.

Josh smirked again.

"I'm serious," Andy insisted.

"You really believe that Santa exists?" Josh asked.

"I don't know," said Andy. "But if he does, he could find a Fat Wheels mountain bike."

"But you just said you don't know if he exists," I said.

"I know," replied Andy, "but *if* he does."

"But he doesn't," said Josh.

"You keep saying that," Andy said. "And I keep saying I know. You guys just don't get it."

"You sure don't." My sister Jessica interrupted us as she dragged a bulging plastic garbage bag into the kitchen.

"Did you hear something?" I asked my friends.

"Feels like a cold wind just blew through here." Josh pretended to shiver.

Jessica ignored him. "Want to know what you guys don't get?"

3

"No," I answered. "But I have a feeling you're going to tell us anyway."

"You're right," Jessica said. "What you guys don't understand is that Christmas isn't about what you *get*. It's about what you *give*."

2

Josh looked across the kitchen table at me. "Maybe you could give your sister."

"To the zoo," added Andy.

I shook my head. "They wouldn't take her."

"You're right," Andy agreed. "She'd scare the little kids."

"I'll tell you what would scare little kids, Andy," Jessica said. "Your *house*."

Andy swiveled around in his chair. "What's wrong with my house?"

"Two things," Jessica said. "One, it's covered with so many big plastic candy canes and Santas and sleds and reindeer that you can hardly see it. Two, when your dad turns on all those Christmas lights at night, you need sunglasses to look at it."

Andy grinned at us. "Every Christmas he wants to have the most lit-up house in town. You should see the electric bill we get in January. It's humongous!"

"Why do you have to have the most lit-up

5

house in town?" Jessica asked. "Since when is Christmas a competition?"

"He does it because he likes to," Andy said with a shrug. "That's all."

"No, that's *not* all," Jessica said. "These days Christmas is all about getting the most and showing it off. Don't you see?"

"The only thing I see is some wacko with a big plastic garbage bag." Josh winked at Andy and me.

"What's in the bag, Jessica?" I asked.

"Coats," my sister answered.

"What for?" asked Andy.

Jessica rolled her eyes. "Haven't you seen the signs all over town? We're having a coat drive. To collect coats for poor people."

"That's a pretty big bag," said Josh. "What did you do? Go door-to-door, asking everyone on the block for their old coats?"

Jessica shook her head. "Believe it or not, I found all these coats in our attic."

"Wait a minute!" I jumped out of my chair, opened the bag, and pulled out a blue parka. "This is mine! I didn't say you could give it away."

"That parka doesn't even fit you," Jessica said. "You haven't worn it in years."

"I don't care," I said. Next I pulled out a green starter's jacket with leather sleeves. "And this one's mine, too! There's no way you're taking it."

"But that jacket's even smaller than the parka," Jessica said.

"Doesn't matter," I replied. "These jackets have memories for me. I was wearing this parka when we rolled those giant snowballs across the street so that the school bus couldn't get through."

Then I picked up the starter's jacket. "And I was wearing this jacket the day we used Amanda Gluck's eyeglasses to burn up ants."

"Oh, my gosh!" Jessica pressed her hands against her cheeks and pretended to be aghast. "How could I be so thick? You wore that jacket when you burned some ants. In that case, we couldn't *possibly* give it to some needy child who'll shiver through the whole winter without a coat."

"Very funny," I said. "Why don't you take your bag of coats and go?"

"With pleasure." Jessica picked up the bag. "It's just really sad that no one ever taught you the true meaning of Christmas, Jake. Christmas is about giving."

"Yeah, well, the only thing you give me is a big pain in the neck," I said.

3

Jessica took the coats to school, and Josh and Andy went home.

I spent the rest of the afternoon going through the ads in the newspaper, looking for stuff to add to my Christmas list.

Just before dinnertime my dad came into the kitchen. I gave him the list.

"That's a lot of things you want, Jake," he said after he read it. "And why did you write down a different store next to each present?"

"I researched and found the best advertised prices," I said. "If you buy each present at the store I've recommended, I guarantee you'll get the lowest price. It's just my way of helping you save money."

"I see," Dad said. "And since you've got fifteen different presents listed here, that could amount to a substantial savings."

"Glad to be of service," I replied proudly. "And by the way, I'd like to remind you that there are only eighteen shopping days left until Christmas. Some of these prices are good only while supplies last. So in order to *really* save money, you might want to do your Christmas shopping sooner rather than later."

"I appreciate the advice," Dad said.

Ha-choo! I sneezed, then blew my nose. "There's one other thing, Dad. I didn't put my new street hockey stick on the list. I was hoping we could get that tonight. The stores will be open late."

Dad frowned. "Street hockey stick?"

"Remember I broke my old one?" I said. "You promised me a new one if I went a whole month without burping out loud at dinner."

"I'm sorry, Jake, but we're all going to visit Aunt Elma tonight," Dad said.

"But what about my hockey stick?" I asked.

"You'll get it for Christmas," Dad said.

"That's not fair!" I protested. "If you wait until Christmas to give it to me, it's going to replace some other present. That means I'll get one less gift than I'm supposed to."

Dad sighed wearily. "Believe me, Jake, you'll still get plenty of gifts. And that reminds me, didn't we just give you a new basketball hoop?"

"But that was for going to school with my shirt tucked in," I argued. "That *really* has nothing to do with Christmas."

Dad pressed his lips together into a hard,

straight line. "You know, Jake, when I was a boy we got gifts only on special occasions. Now it seems you expect something new every week."

"I *have* to," I said.

"You have to?" Dad repeated. "Why?"

"Do you know what would happen to all the toy companies if kids only got stuff at Christmas and on their birthdays?" I asked. "They'd go out of business! Thousands of people would lose their jobs! The whole national economy would suffer. Do you really want that to happen?"

"Well, no. . . . "

"Then you have to keep buying me stuff." I crossed my arms firmly. "It's your responsibility as a citizen of this great country."

Dad smiled. "You're joking, right?"

I was just about to tell him that I was totally serious when Mom came into the kitchen carrying an overnight bag. "Ready to go?"

"Where?" I asked.

"To Aunt Elma's house," she said.

Aunt Elma lived about two hundred miles away in a little town called Heartland. Every year around Christmas we drove to her house and stayed overnight. Aunt Elma baked us homemade cookies and gave us hats and mittens she'd knitted herself. It was the ultimate bore.

"Yeah, great," I moped. "Just what I need, another bright red scarf I'll never wear."

"That's not the point," Mom said. "Aunt Elma has no other family than us. She looks forward to our visit all year. And you're her favorite great-nephew, Jake. If you don't come with us, she'll be very disappointed."

"Hey." I shrugged. "That's life."

But Mom wasn't ready to give up. "It takes her months to knit all those things. And then she spends days cooking."

"Why doesn't she get a membership at the Warehouse Club?" I asked. "It's one-stop shopping. She could buy all that stuff in less than an hour. And they have a special two-day shipping policy. Instead of us going all the way to her house to get that junk, she could ship it here. Think of all the money you'd save on gasoline, Dad."

I took a calculator out of a drawer and quickly figured out how much it would cost to drive the four-hundred-mile round-trip to Heartland and back.

"Just as I suspected," I said. "You'd save enough money to get that new hockey stick you owe me."

"Now I *owe* you a hockey stick?" Dad asked in disbelief.

Jessica came into the kitchen carrying an overnight bag. "I'm ready to go," she said.

Mom and Dad gave her sour looks.

"Uh-oh, something's wrong." Jessica glanced at me. "Let me guess, Jake. You don't want to go to see Aunt Elma."

"And you actually *want* to go?" I asked her.

"Sure."

"Why?" I wanted to know.

"Because Aunt Elma happens to be a very cool person," Jessica replied. "She's practical and sincere, and she isn't totally caught up in materialism like everyone else we know."

"What's materialism?" I asked.

"It's when people believe that the most important thing in their lives is what they own instead of what they think or what they feel," she said.

"I think and feel," I said. "I think going to see Aunt Elma is a drag. And I feel that it'll be a real bummer if I don't get everything on my Christmas list."

"You are totally hopeless." Jessica shook her head sadly.

Meanwhile, Mom and Dad shared a long look. "Are you thinking what I'm thinking?" Mom asked.

Dad nodded. "If he feels this way, maybe we shouldn't bring him."

"If he doesn't go, perhaps he'll discover that he's missing something," Mom said.

Fat chance, I thought.

"He's old enough to stay home alone," Dad said.

"And then we wouldn't have to put Lance in the kennel."

"You're right," Mom agreed.

Dad turned to me. "All right, Jake, if you really don't want to come with us to Aunt Elma's, we'll let you stay home."

I felt my jaw drop. Let me stay home *alone*? Were they *serious*!?

"But I'm warning you," Dad said. "You're going to miss out on some great cookies, and you'll have to take care of Lance."

"That's a deal," I said.

"We expect you to behave yourself," Mom added. "And I expect to come home to a neat and orderly house."

"Definitely," I agreed.

"And you're not allowed to go in my room, or borrow my things, or play any of my CDs," Jessica said. "If you touch *anything* of mine, you'll be really sorry."

"That's the Christmas spirit," I said with a grin.

4

A little while later my parents and sister left for Aunt Elma's house. As soon as they were gone, I called Andy and Josh, but neither of them could come over until the next morning. We made plans to spend the whole day at my house watching movies, playing video games, and eating junk. It was going to be a blast!

That night I stayed up super late watching movies on TV. To be honest, maybe there was a moment or two when I felt bad about not going to see Aunt Elma. But I got over it pretty fast.

When I couldn't keep my eyes open any longer, I went to bed and dreamed about all the cool stuff I was going to get for Christmas. I knew my father was going to try to combine the hockey stick with my other presents, but if I argued hard enough, he would probably give in and get the stick for me separately.

All in all this was shaping up to be the best holiday season ever!

Crunk! The sound of a crash woke me in the middle of the night.

Grooof! Grooof! Lance growled and barked.

I sat up in my bed and rubbed my eyes. Could it have been a dream?

Uhhhnnn . . . I thought I heard someone outside moan.

Lance yipped and scratched excitedly at the door with his paws. He wanted to see what was out there. I went to my bedroom window and looked out into the backyard. It was dark, but in the shadows of the moonlight I thought I saw something. It was partly hidden behind a bush so I couldn't see what it was.

Uhhhnnn . . . There was that moan again. Lance was still scratching at the door. Whoever, or *whatever,* was out there sounded like it was hurt. I got out of bed, pulled on a robe, slipped on my shoes, and left my room.

The house was dark and quiet. For some strange reason I wasn't scared or even nervous. Maybe it was because I was still half-asleep. Anyway, I went to the back door.

Grooof! Lance barked. He wanted to go out with me.

"Sorry, Lance," I said. "It's better if you stay here."

Leaving him in the house, I went out into the backyard. The night air was cold. In the moonlight I saw something that looked exactly like a red and green wave-runner with its nose crushed into the earth. It looked as if it had crash-landed. This was seriously weird. We lived miles away from a lake or river where you could use a wave-runner.

What was it doing in my backyard?

Uhhhnnn . . . Weirder still was the man slumped over the handlebars. He was a big guy, and pretty wide around the middle. I couldn't see much of his face because of the red and green helmet he was wearing, but he did have bright red cheeks and bushy white eyebrows. He was wearing yellow aviator glasses, a brown bomber jacket with white fur trim, and jeans that disappeared into shiny black boots.

Uhhhnnn . . . He turned his face sideways. He had a nasty gash on his nose. He must've gotten it when he crashed. It was bleeding pretty badly.

I hurried back into the house and got the first-aid kit. Then I ran outside again.

When I got out there, the man was standing next to the wave-runner with his back to me.

"Uh, excuse me," I said. "I brought you something for your nose."

The man turned around.

I looked up at his face.

The cut was gone!

5

The man touched his nose with his fingers. His long white beard was pulled tightly into a ponytail. When he saw the first-aid kit in my hand, he said in a deep, friendly voice, "Thank you, Jake. That's a nice gesture, but I won't be needing it."

I stared at him. "How do you know my name?"

"I just do," the man said. He undid the chin strap and pulled the helmet off his head. His hair was long and white. Like his beard, it was pulled into a ponytail.

"What's going on?" I asked. "How did that wave-runner get here?"

"It's a cloud-runner, Jake, not a wave-runner," the man replied. "And it's here because I hired an efficiency expert to see if I could shave some time off my routes. Except I wound up getting so lost and confused that I crashed."

Cloud-runner? Efficiency expert? Routes? What was he talking about?

17

"You're not the only one who's confused," I said.

"Well, it doesn't really matter now," the man said. "The bottom line is, I've had it. This is the last straw. The one that broke the camel's back. Know what I mean?"

"No," I answered.

"It means that I'm through, finished. I quit. You want to know the truth?"

I still wasn't sure what he was talking about, but I said, "Okay."

"Hardly anyone cares about Christmas anymore," said the man. "All they care about is getting presents. And showing off what they've gotten. And keeping up with their neighbors and friends. Every year it's more, more, more."

"Have you been talking to my sister?" I asked.

"Jessica?" the man said. "She's a nice kid, and one of the few who understands. But believe me, Jake, for each one like her, there are a thousand more like you."

Like me? I winced.

The man put his hand on my shoulder. "Sorry, Jake, that was rather blunt. It's just that I've built up fifteen hundred years of frustration, and it's finally coming out."

Fifteen hundred years?

"Er, can I ask you a question?" I said.

"Go ahead," said the man. "Ask anything. It doesn't matter now."

"Okay, so, uh . . . who exactly are you?"

The man stepped back and looked shocked. His hands went up to his face and he felt his ponytail beard. "You don't know?"

I shook my head.

"You don't recognize Santa?" he asked.

6

Time out.

Look, let's be honest.

No kid over the age of five believes in Santa Claus anymore.

The idea that one overweight guy and a bunch of reindeer can deliver all those packages in one night is ridiculous.

I mean, even FedEx finds it hard to stay on schedule at this time of year.

And they've got something like a million jets.

And don't give me that stretching out time nonsense. You know what I'm talking about — that Santa magically stretches out every second into an hour and that's how he gets it all done in one night. That just doesn't cut it.

Besides, if Santa really does exist, why does Toys " Я " Us do such a huge business?

On the other hand, the guy did *look* like Santa . . . sort of.

And I'd heard the crash of that cloud-runner thing.

And that bad cut on his nose had vanished.

"I see that you don't believe me, Jake," the man said.

"Well, uh, I'd *like* to believe you," I stammered. "It's just . . . er, you know . . . kind of a *stretch*."

The man seemed to understand. He didn't look angry or even annoyed.

"Let's see if I can prove it to you," he said. "You probably don't remember much of your life before the age of five, so I'll start there. For your fifth Christmas you got the blue bike with the training wheels. At six, it was the game system. At seven, the bike with the hand brakes. At eight, the whole hockey uniform. At nine, the snowboard. At ten, the second game system. At eleven, the bike with the gear shift. At twelve —"

"Wait a minute," I interrupted him. "How do you know all that?"

"I *told* you," he said. "I'm Santa Claus. Saint Nicholas. Father Christmas. Kris Kringle."

I stared at him uncertainly. How was this possible? There was no such thing as Santa Claus. . . .

Wait a minute! I realized what must have happened. Suddenly it all began to make sense. I was totally awestruck.

"This is truly incredible!" I gasped. "I have to hand it to Jessica and my parents. I really couldn't believe it when they said they were going to let me stay home alone. But now I get it. This whole thing was planned. You must be some teacher from the high school or something. Jessica talked you into pretending to be Santa. You got some friends to dump this busted waverunner in my backyard and you put some fake blood on your nose. It's all a big joke to get me to believe."

I looked around at the trees and bushes in our darkened backyard. "Mom? Dad? Jessica? You guys can come out now. I know you didn't go to Aunt Elma's. You're trying to play a joke and get me to believe Santa Claus really exists because you want me to get into the real spirit of Christmas."

I waited for them to come out from behind a bush or a tree, or from around the side of the house.

But nothing happened.

"Hey, come on," I called to them. "I figured it out, okay? The joke's over."

Still nothing.

"Mom, Dad, tell you what," I said. "You can forget about the hockey stick. Better yet, you can make it one of my Christmas presents. That's fair, isn't it?"

No one answered. No one came out of the shadows.

"Ahem," the man cleared his throat. "There's no one here but us, Jake."

"Nice try, Mr. Whoever-you-are," I said. "But I don't believe you. This *has* to be a trick."

The man tugged thoughtfully at his ponytail beard. "All right, Jake. Let's try something different. Two weeks ago in Mr. Dirksen's class you had a science test. You weren't prepared, as usual, and didn't remember how to compute the density of an object."

I stared at him, amazed. "Wait a minute! You can't know about that. *No one* knows about that!"

"I do," the man said. "When Mr. Dirksen wasn't looking, you peeked at Julia Sax's test. That was very naughty."

I felt my jaw fall.

I'd never told anyone about that.

And that could only mean one thing.

I swallowed. "Are you . . . from the Psychic Pals Hotline?"

The man looked disgusted. "*That* is an insult, Jake. How can you believe in that cheap, phony TV show and not believe in me?"

"Well, at least it's on TV," I said. "You're not."

The man glowered angrily at me. I realized I'd just dissed him pretty bad.

"Gee, I'm sorry, really," I said.

The man still glared at me. He wasn't faking it. He was peeved.

I started to feel light-headed.

I know it's hard to believe. . . .

But there was no way anyone not associated

with the Psychic Pals Hotline could have known that I cheated on that test.

My heart started to beat hard. My throat felt tight. I swallowed nervously. "So, uh, I guess that means you're really, uh, Santa Claus?"

"I *was*," he grumbled.

7

Santa got back on the wave-runner, or cloud-runner, or whatever it was.

"Wait a minute," I said. "You just spent all that time trying to convince me that you're Santa Claus . . . and now you're leaving?"

"I told you, Jake," he said. "I've had enough. I'm tired of the whole darn thing. The manufacturing hassles, the delivery schedules, the climate . . . "

"Climate?" I repeated uncertainly.

"The North Pole," he sputtered. "Snow and ice three hundred sixty-five days a year. I'm going where it's warm and dry. I've heard good things about the Las Vegas area. The climate is supposed to be great, the cost of living is low, and the casinos have those all-you-can-eat buffets."

I couldn't believe what I was hearing! Santa was going to quit being Santa and move to Las Vegas?

"You can't quit," I said.

"Oh, no? Watch me." Santa pressed a button on the handlebar of the cloud-runner. The engine made a clicking sound but wouldn't start. A red warning light glowed on the display panel.

"Come on!" Santa mumbled. He pressed the button again, and again the engine made the clicking sound. The red light continued to glow.

"Oh, well." Santa got off the cloud-runner. "At least it's still under warranty."

He reached into the bomber jacket and pulled out a gray cell phone. He punched in a number and the phone made a lot of beeps. Then he pressed it against his ear.

"Hello?" he said. "Hello, is anyone there?"

I noticed a small red light glowing on the phone. "I hate to say this, Santa, but I think your battery's low."

Santa pulled the phone away from his ear and stared at it. "Darn it." He closed the cell phone. "Used to be, the only thing that glowed red was Rudolph's nose. Now my whole life is full of glowing red lights."

"You could use the phone in my house if you want," I offered.

"That's nice of you, Jake. Thanks, I will," he said.

We started to walk across the backyard.

"Could you just do me one favor?" I asked.

"Like what?" Santa said.

"Could you not stay on the phone too long?" I

said. "My dad gets mad at us when we make long-distance phone calls."

"I understand," Santa said.

We got to the back door and I opened it to let Santa in. Suddenly I heard rapid thumping coming down the hall toward us.

It was Lance!

I'd forgotten about him!

He didn't like strangers!

8

L ance bounded toward us. I tried to block his path, but he got around me and headed for Santa.

Oh, great! I was about to become the kid who let his dog maul Santa Claus!

Lance jumped up . . . and started to lick Santa's face.

"Hello, Lance, my old friend," Santa chuckled. "Nice to see you again. Now be good and get down."

Lance got back down on all fours. He wagged his tail happily and grinned with his tongue hanging out.

Santa patted him on the head. "That's a nice dog."

I didn't get it. Why wasn't Lance growling? Why was he sitting happily at Santa's feet?

"So you remember," Santa said with a smile. He reached into the pocket of his bomber jacket and pulled out a dog biscuit. "Here you go."

He tossed the biscuit in the air. Lance caught it and headed off to a corner, chewing happily.

"How does Lance know you?" I asked.

Santa gave me a look. "Get with the program, Jake. He sees me every Christmas."

"Oh, uh . . . yeah." I was still finding this whole Santa thing pretty tough to believe.

Santa looked around. "The telephone?"

"Right." I led him into the kitchen.

Santa dialed a phone number and waited while it rang. He put his hand over the receiver. "It gets pretty hectic at this time of year. Sometimes it takes them a while to answer."

Someone must've answered because Santa started to speak. "I had a little problem with that cloud-runner . . . Yes, I'm okay, but you're going to have to send someone to get me. . . . What? Why so long? . . . Sure, the pickup truck will be fine. . . . The list? I've only checked it once. . . . Of course I know I have to check it twice. . . . Hmmm, good point. Hold on."

Santa put his hand over the receiver again. "Jake, is your dad's fax machine hooked up?"

I started to ask how he knew my dad had a fax machine. Then I realized it was a pretty silly question. If Santa knew about my science test, he could know about my dad's fax machine. "Yes, I'm pretty sure he got a fax this morning."

"Good." Santa spoke into the phone again. "You can fax the list to me here. . . . Yes, the Sherman residence in Jeffersonville. . . . Right. And hurry."

Santa hung up. "Thanks for letting me use the phone, Jake. Would you mind if I sat here at the kitchen table? I've got an awful lot to do."

"Uh, okay."

"You wouldn't happen to have any hot chocolate, would you?" Santa asked. "I sure could use some right now."

"I think we have some," I said. "I'll make it for you."

"That would be nice," Santa said. He took off the bomber jacket and hung it over the back of a kitchen chair. Underneath he was wearing a red and green plaid shirt.

I was in the middle of making the hot chocolate when I heard the fax ring in my dad's office.

"I'll get it." Santa got up and left the kitchen. As I watched him walk away, I noticed that he did have a pretty big belly. But his butt wasn't bad at all. It was nothing like the major bubble butt Josh had said he'd have.

A few moments later Santa came back with a long scroll of white fax paper.

"Here's the first part of it," he said, sitting down at the kitchen table again.

"Is that the list of the presents everyone wants?" I asked hopefully.

"Oh, no, Jake," he said. "I already *know* what everyone wants. This is the list of who's been naughty and who's been nice. You know, the one I always check twice."

He took off the aviator glasses and put on a pair of black-rimmed reading glasses. Then he took out a pen and started to go down the list. By now I'd finished making the hot chocolate. I put the steaming mug on the table beside him. As I did, I looked over his shoulder. On the fax paper were long columns of names.

"Thanks, Jake, that's very nice of you." Santa took a sip of hot chocolate. "You wouldn't happen to have a gingerbread cookie around, would you?"

"Sure do," I said. Mom always got us gingerbread cookies at this time of year. I went to the cupboard and brought the package back to the table.

"Extremely nice of you, Jake. Thanks." Santa picked up a cookie and took a bite.

"Could I, uh, ask a question?" I said.

"Sure, Jake, anything," Santa replied.

"If you're really quitting, how come you're still working on the list?"

Santa's bushy white eyebrows rose in surprise. "Oh, uh, well you can't simply quit and walk away from the job. I mean, you have to finish what you start, Jake. I can't just drop everything and leave a big mess."

That made sense . . . sort of.

"Another question?" I asked.

"Go ahead."

"How come you put your hair and beard in ponytails?"

"Convenience, Jake," Santa replied. "This way the beard doesn't get full of crumbs when I eat. And my hair doesn't get in the way when I'm on the move."

"You won't look like that on Christmas, will you?" I asked.

Santa gave me a sad look. "By Christmas I'll have short hair and no beard at all, Jake. I'll be sitting by a pool somewhere in Vegas. You don't really think I want to go through the rest of my life with people constantly telling me I look like Santa Claus, do you?"

"I guess not," I answered and scuffed my shoe nervously on the floor. There was *one last* question I was dying to ask.

Santa looked over his reading glasses at me. "Is there something else, Jake?"

"There's this one last question," I said. "But I don't want you to be insulted."

"Go ahead and ask," Santa said.

I swallowed hard and got up my nerve. "Well, I was just wondering . . . what happened to your butt?"

9

The ridges in Santa's broad forehead furrowed. "What's wrong with my butt?"

"It's like . . . nonexistent," I said. "I mean, I have this friend who said you'd have a mighty big one."

Santa nodded. "You must be talking about Josh Hopka."

He knew? Josh would kill me if he found out I'd ratted on him. "You can't tell him I told you!"

"Relax, Jake," Santa said. "I already knew he said that. The funny thing is, Josh was right. I *used to* have a big butt. Then a couple of Christmases ago I got back to the North Pole and discovered an extra *Buns of Steel* videotape at the bottom of my bag. All it took was twenty minutes a day, four times a week, and good-bye bubble butt. In fact, I just sent away for *Abs of Iron*. I'm going to work on my stomach next. After fifteen hundred years of flab, I want that hard-body look."

"Cool," I said.

Santa went back to checking the list. It was still the middle of the night and I felt pretty sleepy, so I went back to bed.

The next thing I knew, it was morning and the doorbell was ringing.

Ding dong!

"Just a minute!" I yawned and got out of bed and pulled on my robe. I left my room and headed toward the front of the house. As I passed the kitchen I noticed that Santa was still sitting at the table. Two more long scrolls of white fax paper were spread out in front of him.

I went to the door. "Who is it?"

"Josh and Andy, who do you think?" Josh called back.

"Oh, right." I'd forgotten they were coming over. I pulled the door open. When Josh and Andy saw me, they looked puzzled.

"How come you're still in your pajamas?" Andy asked.

"I, uh, didn't get much sleep last night." I yawned again and scratched my nose.

Josh and Andy went past me and into the house. "You stayed up late watching TV?"

"And I got up in the middle of the night," I said.

"Jake?" Santa called from the kitchen.

"Yeah?"

"Could you come here for a second?"

"Sure," I called back, then turned to my friends. "Just wait here, guys."

I went into the kitchen. Santa was poring over one of the faxes lined with names.

"What's the latest on this Barry Dunn character?" Santa asked, tapping his pen on the list. "Has he changed at all?"

"What do you mean?" I asked.

"He's been on my naughty list ever since I can remember," Santa said. "Since this is my last year as Santa, I was hoping that something might have changed."

Barry Dunn was your basic dirtbag bully. He'd tried to beat me up when I switched bodies with Mr. Braun, my muscular gym teacher. But thanks to my brains and Mr. Braun's muscles, we'd managed to outsmart him.

"I hate to say this, Santa, but Barry Dunn is just as demented as he's always been," I said.

"Oh, well, thanks for being honest." Santa made an "X" on the list next to Barry's name.

I went back to the living room where Andy and Josh were waiting.

"Who's that?" Josh asked.

"Santa," I said. "He crashed his cloud-runner in the backyard last night. It's pretty much wrecked, so he had to set up a temporary office in the kitchen while he waits for someone to come get him. He was just asking me whether I thought Barry Dunn was naughty or nice."

Josh and Andy stared at me like I'd lost my mind.

"Jake, are you feeling okay?" Josh asked.

"Sure." I yawned again. "I'm just a little tired, that's all."

"That's *all*?" Andy repeated.

"Except that you think Santa Claus is sitting in your kitchen," Josh said.

"Yeah, he's checking the list for the second time," I said.

"What list?" Andy asked.

"The list of who's been naughty or nice," I said. "I just told you. That's why he asked me about Barry Dunn."

Josh and Andy craned their necks to look into the kitchen.

"I have news for you, Jake," Josh said in a low voice. "I don't know who that guy is, but he's not Santa Claus."

"How do you know?" I asked.

"Three reasons," Josh answered. "First, Santa Claus does not exist. Second, that guy isn't wearing a Santa suit. And third, he doesn't have a Santa butt."

"He's been working out to the *Buns of Steel* video," I explained. "Just twenty minutes a day, four times a week. And he only wears the suit at Christmas."

Andy and Josh craned their necks and looked into the kitchen again.

Then they looked at each other.

Then they looked at me.

"You said something about him crashing into your backyard last night?" Andy said.

"Right."

"This," Josh said, "I have to see."

10

We went outside and around to the back of the house.

"Are you sure it's okay to leave that stranger sitting at your kitchen table?" Andy asked.

"He's not a stranger," I said. "He's Santa Claus."

"Give me a break, Jake," said Josh. "Since when do you believe in Santa?"

"Since he got here last night," I replied simply. I really didn't want to tell them how he knew about the science test I'd cheated on.

We walked across the backyard and stopped at the crashed vehicle.

"It's a wave-runner," Josh said.

"Santa says it's a cloud-runner." I told them about hearing the crash the night before and finding Santa slumped over the handlebars.

"Look," Josh said impatiently. "I don't care *who* you think that guy is, or what you say happened last night, this thing is *still* a wave-runner."

"Then how did it get in my backyard?" I asked.

Josh looked around, but didn't say anything.

"Jake has a good point," Andy said. "There's no water anywhere near here."

"Then it's obvious that somebody brought it here," Josh said.

"How?" I asked.

"They must have carried it," said Josh.

I pointed at the cloud-runner. "Look at that thing. It must weigh a ton. He couldn't have carried it alone."

"He had help," Josh said.

"Then explain this to me," I said. "Why would a bunch of guys carry a smashed-up wave-runner into my backyard in the middle of the night? And why would one of them stay behind and pretend to be Santa? And why does he just happen to have long white hair and a long white beard? *And* why is he getting these humongous lists full of names faxed to my house?"

Once again Josh looked around and didn't say anything. Andy scratched his head thoughtfully. A cold breeze shook the bare branches of the trees and went right through my robe. I pulled it tight and stuck my hands in the pockets.

"Can we go back inside?" I asked. "It's a little cold to be out here in pajamas and a robe."

We started back toward the house.

"Okay, let's forget about the wave-runner for a

second," Andy said. "How do you know that guy in your kitchen isn't just faking it?"

I told him how Santa knew every Christmas present I'd ever gotten, plus he knew about naughty stuff that no one else in the whole world knew about.

"Like what?" Josh asked.

I could see I had no choice, so I told him how I'd cheated on Mr. Dirksen's science test a few weeks before.

"I knew it!" Josh cried. "I kept wondering how you aced that test, you slimeball."

"Who's calling who a slimeball?" I said. "You cheat all the time!"

"Do not!" Josh insisted.

"Oh, yeah? What about that vocabulary test?" I asked. "You and Amber Sweeney were the only kids in the class who knew what carbuncle meant. And it just so happens that you sit right behind her."

"Yeah? So?" Josh huffed.

"Don't tell me you didn't look at her paper," I said.

"No way," said Josh.

"You swear?" I asked. "Cross your heart and hope to die?"

Josh crossed his heart. "Happy?"

"I still don't believe you," I said.

"Can we get back to the real issue here?" Andy interrupted us. "This isn't about cheating on tests. This is about figuring out if the guy with the buns of steel in Jake's kitchen is really Santa or not."

"Will you come off it?" Josh scoffed. "The guy's a fake."

"Maybe," Andy said. "But I'd still like to hear all the reasons Jake thinks he's real. Is there anything else you haven't told us, Jake?"

"Lance acts like he knows him," I said. "It turns out that Santa brings him a dog biscuit every year. When Santa showed up last night, Lance sat down and acted like he knew a dog biscuit was coming."

"Give me a break," Josh snickered. "That doesn't mean diddly squat."

I held the door open for my friends and we went back into the house.

"I'm glad you're back, Jake," Santa called from the kitchen. "Could you come in here for a moment?"

This time Josh and Andy came with me into the kitchen. The table was covered with more long sheets of fax paper. Some of them hung over the edge and down to the floor.

"Hello, Andy," Santa said with a smile. But when he turned to Josh, he didn't smile. "Hello, Josh."

"Uh, hi," Josh and Andy replied uncertainly.

"Jake may have told you that I'm going over this year's list for the second time," Santa said.

"It's a little difficult to remember every boy and girl, so I sometimes ask for help. Do any of you know Adam Egan?"

"He's on my basketball team," Andy said.

"What's your opinion of him?" Santa asked.

"My opinion?" Andy repeated uncertainly.

"Naughty or nice?" Santa asked.

"Well . . . " Andy rubbed his chin. "He seems okay. I mean, he doesn't showboat or anything on the court. And he dishes the ball off when he doesn't have an open shot. So, yeah, I guess I'd say he's nice."

"Good." Santa made a check mark next to Adam's name.

"Uh, could I interrupt for a second?" Josh said.

"Yes, Josh, how can I help you?" Santa asked.

"How do you know my name?" Josh asked.

Santa looked surprised. "Didn't Jake tell you?"

"Well, yes, but, I mean, how can you be Santa Claus?" Josh asked.

"It's a dirty job filled with big fat Santa butts and slimy green Christmas boogers, but someone has to do it," Santa replied.

Josh turned red.

Santa looked at Andy. "Would you mind going into Jake's dad's office and seeing if they've faxed any more of the list?"

"Sure," Andy said.

As soon as Andy left, Santa put his hands together and looked up at Josh. "Green Christmas boogers? Really, Josh, isn't that a bit infantile?"

Josh bit his lip. He'd just been dissed big time. "Wait a minute. How do I know Jake didn't rat on me?"

"Let's see, Josh." Santa tugged pensively on his beard. "You didn't get your first bike until you were seven. When you were eight you got the knock hockey set. At the age of nine you threw a football into the Christmas tree and, as a punishment, didn't get your Rollerblades until two weeks later."

Josh's jaw dropped.

"In the bottom drawer of your dresser, behind the green crewneck sweater you hate, is a half-finished bag of chocolate kisses you're not supposed to have," Santa went on. "Your next-door neighbor's cat, Tornado, howls at night and keeps you awake. So two weeks ago you mixed red-hot sauce into some chopped meat and tried to get Tornado to eat it. Fortunately, the cat had more sense than that."

Josh blinked and turned even redder than before.

Santa wagged a finger at him. "Naughty, naughty."

Josh's eyes bulged out.

"Is there anything else?" I asked.

Santa frowned. "Like what, Jake?"

"Maybe some naughty stuff Josh did at school," I suggested.

"Oh, yes," Santa remembered. "That vocabulary test. The one where you copied Amber Sweeney's answers."

I turned to Josh, who had gone from bright red to white as a sheet. "Cross your heart and hope to die?"

"H-h-how could you kn-know about that test?" Josh asked in a quavering voice.

Just then Andy came back into the kitchen with a long sheet of fax paper. "Listen, Santa, I know this isn't any of my business, but you see this guy Zack Elkund? We went to summer camp with him last year and he's really bad news."

"I appreciate the tip, Andy." Santa made a mark on the list next to Zack's name.

Andy grinned. "Hey, this is really cool."

Then he noticed that Josh looked pale and was trembling.

"Something wrong?" Andy asked him.

Josh nodded slowly. "I think we have a major problem."

11

Andy and I looked around the kitchen for the "major problem" Josh was talking about. Except for Santa and his list, I didn't see anything out of the ordinary.

"What's the problem?" Andy asked Josh.

Josh gestured at Santa. "I have a feeling he's the real thing."

"Why's that a problem?" Andy asked.

"Because if he's really Santa and that's really the list, then we aren't getting anything this year," Josh said.

Andy grinned. "Maybe *you're* not getting anything, Mr. Green Christmas Booger, but *my* conscience is clear."

"Hey, Santa," Josh said. "How about Andy? Has he been naughty or nice?"

"Let's see." Santa pressed one finger alongside of his nose and gazed upward. "Back in September, Andy, you found someone's wallet on the street near your house."

"Right," Andy said. "And I put it in a mailbox so that it would get returned to its owner."

"That sounds pretty nice," I said.

"Except for the two dollars he removed from it first," Santa added.

Now it was Andy who turned red.

Josh grinned. "Naughty, naughty, Andy."

"Wait." Andy recovered. "I, er, considered that a finder's fee."

Santa raised a dubious eyebrow.

"What were you saying about having a clear conscience?" Josh asked.

"I say it was a finder's fee," Andy maintained. "Come on, Santa, give me a break. You know that was the only thing I've done that was even questionable."

"Smashing pumpkins on Halloween?" Santa asked.

"But it was Halloween," Andy said.

"The prank phone calls?"

"*Every* kid does that," said Andy.

"Letting all the crickets loose in Mr. Dirksen's lab?"

"Animal rights!" Andy exclaimed.

Santa tugged thoughtfully at his beard. "Andy, just because you can come up with excuses doesn't make what you did right."

Josh wagged his finger at Andy. "Tsk, tsk."

Andy's shoulders sagged. "Does that mean I'm *not* gonna get anything this Christmas?"

46

Santa sat back and crossed his arms. "I'm not sure, Andy. Since this is the last Christmas I'll ever do this, I'm inclined to be a bit easier on you boys."

Andy sighed with relief. "Thanks, Santa, I won't forget this, man. You are A-okay with me."

But Josh looked upset. "Wait, Santa. What do you mean this is the *last* Christmas you'll ever do this?"

"Santa's quitting," I told them.

12

Andy and Josh looked stunned.

"Why?" Andy asked.

"Because no one over the age of five believes in him anymore," I said. "And nobody cares about Christmas spirit. All they care about is getting presents."

"That's not true!" Andy insisted.

"Oh, really?" Santa said. "Let's see, Andy. There's the Turbo game system, the snowboard, the Bubonic Plague CD, and the Sky Walk basketball shoes. Unless, of course, I'm forgetting something."

"Well, yeah, you forgot the Fat Wheels mountain bike," Andy said. "I wasn't going to ask for it because I didn't think you existed. But now that I know you really exist, I'm kind of hoping you could throw the bike in, too."

Josh poked him in the ribs.

"Hey! What was that for?" Andy cried.

"First you tell Santa it's not true that all we

care about is getting presents," Josh said. "Then when he reminds you of all the presents you want, you actually have the nerve to *add* one!"

"Well, *you* asked for a Fat Wheels mountain bike," Andy sniffed. "So why can't I get one, too?"

"See what I mean, boys?" Santa asked.

"Listen, Santa, you can't quit," Josh said desperately. "It's totally, completely unfair."

Santa's broad forehead wrinkled. "That's a surprising statement, especially coming from *you*, Josh. Why did you say it?"

"Because now that I know you're real, I *want* to believe in you," Josh said.

Andy and I nodded in agreement.

"He's right, Santa," I said. "For all these years I couldn't believe in you because I was afraid everyone would make fun of me."

"And it's not like you gave us a lot of evidence that you existed," Andy added. "You could've done a little better in that department, you know."

"You mean, I should have shown myself to the whole world?" Santa replied. He pointed at the long sheets of fax paper spilling off the kitchen table. "Just imagine what my Christmas list would look like then. It would be ten times the size it is now." He shook his head. "No, what I needed was for people to believe in me because they believed in Christmas. But except for a few people like Jake's sister, Jessica, hardly anyone your age believes anymore."

49

"That goody-two-shoes," Josh grumbled.

"I still think this is a credibility issue," Andy said. "Maybe you need help, Santa. Have you ever thought that this could be a public relations problem? I bet a good PR person could spruce up your image."

"I'm quite content with my image, thank you," Santa said with a huff. Then he held up a bunch of fax paper. "Look at this. Thousands of kids who *want* things. But have any of them thought about what they want to *give*? Have you boys thought about it?"

"I wouldn't mind giving Jessica a fat lip," Josh muttered.

"Hey, great Christmas spirit," Andy cracked.

"So?" Santa asked.

Andy, Josh, and I shared a guilty look.

The truth was, none of us had given any thought at all to what we wanted to give.

13

Josh, Andy, and I shared a dismal look. None of us felt very good at that moment.

"Everything he said is true," Josh said.

"We think only about ourselves and what we want for Christmas," I said.

Josh turned to Santa. "I'd probably want to quit, too, if I were in your shoes."

A feeling of gloom fell over the room. It was hard to believe that all those centuries of Christmas, and all that cheer and joy, were ending right at my kitchen table.

Suddenly, Andy brightened. "Wait, I have an idea! Listen, Santa, suppose we promise to be better in the future? Would that change your mind?"

"How do I know you'll keep your word?" Santa asked.

"You can keep an eye on us," Andy said.

"But I'm going to be lounging by a pool in Las Vegas," Santa said.

"No, no, the whole idea is you won't quit," Andy said. "You can keep being Santa. This year you'll give us all the stuff we want. Then next year, if we're not good, you don't have to give us anything."

Santa slowly shook his head. "I'm sorry, Andy, but I'm not making any deals. I'm not interested in seeing how you behave *after* you know that Santa is real. Because no matter how well you act, I'll always wonder if you're only doing it in order to get more presents."

Andy bowed his head in disappointment. None of us knew what to say. Josh shoved his hands into his pockets. I stared at the floor.

"I have to get back to work," Santa said. "Would one of you do me a favor and go see if any more of the list has come over the fax machine?"

"Sure." I went into my dad's office. Another four or five feet of fax paper had come through. I also noticed a long red streak on the edge of the paper.

I brought the fax back into the kitchen and gave it to Santa. "Looks like our supply of fax paper is about to run out," I said.

Santa pursed his lips. "Is there any place where you can get fax paper on a Sunday around here?"

"Just the mall," Josh said.

"Would you boys mind going over there and getting me some?" Santa asked.

"No problem," I said.

"It's the least we could do," added Josh.

"Yeah," Andy agreed. "And while we're there we can check out that new virtual ski racing game. I hear they're gonna come out with a home version next year. I'm definitely gonna want it for next Chris — "

Andy stopped talking when he noticed that Josh and I were staring daggers at him. He quickly corrected himself. "Uh, I meant, I'm definitely gonna want to *give* that game to someone next Christmas."

Josh rolled his eyes disgustedly. "Yeah, right, Andy. Now come on, let's go before you manage to squeeze *both* feet into your mouth."

Josh and Andy started to leave the kitchen, but I stayed behind.

"Aren't you coming, Jake?" Josh asked.

"In a second," I said. "But first I want to talk to Santa alone."

14

Josh left the kitchen, but Andy hesitated and looked back at Santa and me.

"Don't try to make any last-minute deals with Santa," he warned me. "Like trying to get him to take stuff away from us and give it to you."

Josh reached back through the doorway, grabbed Andy by the collar, and yanked him out.

Bang! The kitchen door slammed shut.

Santa folded his hands together. "What did you want to say, Jake?"

"Listen, Santa, I know I can't stop you from quitting," I said. "But I feel really bad about this. I mean, what about all the little kids who still believe in you?"

"They'll believe in me no matter what," Santa replied.

"Yeah, but, I mean, I feel like you're quitting just because of Josh, Andy, and me," I said. "Like it's all our fault."

"I don't mean to make you feel that way," Santa

said. "I crashed into your backyard by accident, Jake. It could just as easily have been someone else's yard. Then I would probably be sitting in some other boy's kitchen and you'd never know about it."

"But it *is* my kitchen," I said. "And I'll probably go through the rest of my life feeling horrible because I'll know I was the guy who couldn't talk Santa out of quitting."

"Believe me, Jake, it's not your fault," Santa said.

I nodded sadly and started to leave. But then I had a thought and stopped. "Being Santa can't be a *total* drag, can it? I mean, there must be *some* rewards involved."

Santa thought for a moment. He drummed his fingers over the pile of lists spread out on the table.

"All right, Jake," he said, as if he'd decided something. "Maybe you're right." He snapped his fingers like a magician doing a card trick. Out of nowhere, a small red and green envelope appeared in his hand. He held it out to me.

"What is it?" I asked.

"An idea I just had," he said. "Take it with you to the mall. But promise me you won't open it until you get there."

"I promise," I said.

15

I went into my room and changed clothes. Then I went outside. Josh and Andy were waiting in my driveway.

"What took you so long?" Andy asked.

"I had to get dressed," I said.

Andy squinted at me suspiciously. "Are you *sure* you didn't make some kind of deal with Santa?"

"Yes, I'm sure," I said. "But what if I did? What's the big deal?"

"Are you serious?" Andy asked. "Why should you get more presents than Josh or me?"

"Didn't you learn anything from what just happened in my kitchen?" I asked. "Why are you still being so selfish?"

"I'm not being selfish," Andy said. "I just don't want you to get more presents than me."

I stared at him in wonder. He *still* didn't get it.

We started to walk toward the mall. Josh trudged along slowly with his head bowed and his hands jammed in his pockets. He looked really bummed.

"Hey, what's wrong?" I asked.

"I keep wondering if he's quitting because of me," he said. "I mean, all that stuff about Santa butts and green Christmas boogers. He must be really mad."

"You're right, Josh," Andy said. "Maybe if you go back and tell him you don't want any presents, he'll change his mind and keep being Santa."

"Cut it out, Andy," I said. "Why don't *you* go back and tell him you don't want any presents?"

"Are you kidding?" Andy sputtered. "This may be Santa's last year. I'm gonna take everything I can get."

Since it was a Sunday and only eighteen days from Christmas, some of my neighbors were putting Christmas lights and decorations on their lawns and houses.

"Oh, wow!" Josh stopped and pointed at one house. "Look at that!"

The owner of the house had put a big red and white plastic display of Santa, his sled, and reindeer on his roof. In addition, the roof, chimney, windows, and all the bushes in the yard were covered with lights. The front door was encircled by the biggest wreath I'd ever seen! People could actually walk through it. Huge plastic candy canes, snowmen, angels, and candles were propped up on the front lawn.

"I'm going to have to warn my dad about this guy," Andy said. "He may actually have more stuff on his house than we do."

"I thought Christmas wasn't supposed to be about competing," I said.

"It's not," said Andy. "But I know my dad. He still doesn't want anyone to have more lights than we do."

The kid was hopeless.

"Come on, Andy." I tugged at his sleeve. "Let's go to the mall."

We left my neighborhood and started along the main road through town. Ahead of us a long line of people waited in front of a church. A lot of the people in line were wearing old coats with holes and stains. Their shoes were scuffed and worn thin. Some of the men had dark stubble on their faces.

"Know what this is?" Josh said. "It's a food line. The church gives out free food to needy people."

Andy took a deep sniff. "Hey, it smells pretty good. And I'm kind of hungry. I could use something to eat."

"It's not for us, dummy," Josh said. "It's for people who can't afford a meal."

Then I had an idea. "Know what we should do? We should ask if we can help."

"Why?" Andy asked.

"Because it would be a way of giving something without expecting anything in return," I said. "It would show that we're in the Christmas spirit."

"But what about Santa's fax paper?" Josh asked.

"Let's find out if the church needs us," I said. "If they do, we can hurry up and get Santa his fax paper and then come back here and help."

We continued down the line of people until we arrived at some long tables. On the tables were bags of bread and big pots of steaming hot soup. On the other side of the table a bunch of church workers were helping to serve the hungry people.

Andy stopped and pointed at a church worker who was giving out cups of hot chocolate. "Isn't that Alex Silver?"

The guy was wearing a knit cap pulled low on his head. But I noticed a tiny diamond stud earring in his ear.

"You're right, Andy," I said. "I can't believe it!"

16

Alex Silver was our friend . . . sort of. Sometimes we played basketball with him. But at other times he acted too cool for us. At the beginning of eighth grade he and I had decided to call ourselves the Knights of Wedgy. We'd planned to rule Burt Itchupt Middle School and wedgy everyone who disrespected us. Instead I got stuck in the first day of school until I figured out that being cool wasn't about picking on other kids.

We went over to the hot chocolate table. "Alex, is that really you?" I asked.

Alex looked up. "Jake, my man! How's it going?"

"What are you doing here?" Andy asked.

Alex looked puzzled. "What does it *look* like I'm doing?"

"But this isn't even your religion," Josh said.

"Since when does helping people have anything to do with what religion you are?" Alex asked. He gave each of us a cup of hot chocolate and poured one for himself. He shivered a little as he sipped the creamy brew.

"Are you wearing your cap low because you don't want anyone to recognize you?" Andy asked him.

"No way," Alex said. "The reason my hat's pulled low is because it's cold. I've been out here since six this morning."

"You do this every year?" I asked.

"I've donated my time every year since second grade," Alex said. A long white plume of vapor escaped his lips.

Josh, Andy, and I shared a look. I knew what my friends were thinking. Who would have thought that Alex Silver would be working at a soup kitchen?

"So listen, Alex," Josh said. "You think maybe we could help, too?"

"Sure." Alex pointed at a heavyset woman wearing white earmuffs and a red ski parka. "You should talk to Sister Elizabeth."

Alex went back to serving hot chocolate, and we went over to Sister Elizabeth.

"Excuse me," Josh said to her. "We were wondering if you needed any more volunteers."

"It's very nice of you boys to offer," she said, "but right now we have all the volunteers we need. At this time of year it seems like everyone wants to help. But we serve the needy all year long. I know you boys are in school during the week, but maybe you'd like to help on Saturday mornings in April and May."

April and May?

"I would," Josh said, "but I always have baseball."

"And I'm going out for spring soccer," I said.

We both looked at Andy because we knew he wasn't doing any sports in the spring.

"Hey, don't look at me," Andy said. "I always sleep late on Saturday mornings."

"It's funny how people always want to volunteer around Christmas when the weather's cold and there isn't much to do," Sister Elizabeth said. "But very few people are willing to give up their weekend mornings when the weather gets nice."

Josh, Andy, and I shared another guilty look.

"Don't feel bad, boys," Sister Elizabeth said. "At least you were willing to volunteer. But perhaps you should ask yourselves why you want to help. Is it because you really want to bring comfort to others, or is it because you want to make *yourselves* feel better?"

17

Josh, Andy, and I left the church and waved good-bye to Alex. We had just started toward the mall again when we heard loud arguing coming from a parking lot filled with hundreds of Christmas trees for sale. In the middle of the lot, two men were having a tug-of-war over one tree.

"I saw it first!" one of them shouted as he pulled at the top of the tree.

"No, I did!" yelled the other as he pulled at the base of the tree.

A man wearing a red and black plaid coat was trying to break up the argument. "You don't have to fight over this tree," he said. "I've got hundreds for sale."

"But I want this one!" both men yelled at the same time.

Crack! The tree broke. Both men fell backward, still clutching parts of it in their hands.

"Now look what you did, you stupid jerk!" one of them yelled.

"Me?" shouted the other. "I didn't do it. It's all your fault, you bonehead!"

The two men started to push and shove each other. Meanwhile, the man wearing the red and black plaid coat shrugged helplessly and turned away.

"That was dumb," Andy said. "Now *neither* of them will get the tree they wanted."

"He's learning," Josh said, winking at me.

"Wait a minute, guys," Andy protested. "That was one isolated incident. Most people don't act like that."

When we finally got to the mall, it was one huge traffic jam.

"Can you believe this?" Josh asked as we walked across the parking lot. "There are cars *everywhere!*"

He was right. I'd never seen the parking lot so full. Not only was every space filled, but they were parking on the grass and in the no-parking fire zones as well.

Screech! From behind us came the sound of a car skidding. We spun around. Two cars were both trying to get into the same parking space.

Honk! Honk! Honk! Both drivers honked their horns and rolled down their windows.

"I saw this spot first!" shouted a lady with red hair.

"No way!" yelled the other driver. "I saw it first! So back off!"

"No, *you* back off!" the red-haired lady shouted.

"Guess that's just another one of those 'isolated' incidents," Josh quipped.

"You're a laugh and a half, Josh," Andy muttered.

We went into the mall. I'd never seen it so crowded! People were jammed shoulder to shoulder, lugging shopping bags and pushing baby strollers.

"Hold it, guys!" Andy stopped and took a deep sniff. "Smell that? Fresh baked chocolate-chip cookies!"

Andy took off toward a cookie shop. Meanwhile a mother pulling a crying little kid by the hand passed Josh and me.

"If you don't stop crying I'm going to tell Santa not to give you anything for Christmas!" the mother yelled.

"Don't, Momma! Don't tell Santa! *Please!*" the kid screamed and started to cry even harder.

A father and his daughter came by.

"I don't *care* if Jenny Taylor has Brain Surgeon Barbie," the father growled. "You can't have everything everybody else has."

"Why not?" his daughter asked.

"Because we're not made of money," said the father.

"Then how come you have a boat, a snowmobile, a motorcycle, and a jet ski?" the daughter asked.

"That's different," the father grumbled.

Josh seemed shaken. "Know what's weird? I never looked at it like this before. This is really wacked, Jake. It's definitely *not* what Christmas is supposed to be about."

"That reminds me." I took the red and green envelope out of my pocket. "Santa gave me this just before we left my house. He said I wasn't supposed to open it until I got to the mall."

Josh stared warily at the envelope. "You *sure* you want to open it?"

"Why not?" I tore it open. "You don't think Santa would do anything mean, do you?"

Inside the envelope was a small white card. On it was a message written in large, looping letters.

"What's it say?" Josh asked.

I read the card: "Congratulations, Jake. You're Santa."

Whump!

18

I'd heard that *whump!* before. It was the same sound Mr. Dirksen's intelligence transfer machine made when it switched people into different bodies.

Josh was staring at me. His eyes were bugging out. "Oh, no!" he cried.

Instinctively, my hand went to my face. But it wasn't *my* face anymore! It was a fat face with fleshy cheeks and a round nose! And a long white beard! And long white hair!

I looked down, but I couldn't see my feet. A big, round belly I'd never had before was blocking my view. And it was covered by a bright red jacket with gold buttons and white trim! And a wide black leather belt!

I wiggled my toes, and felt them rub against the insides of the stiff leather Santa boots I was now wearing.

Andy came back through the crowd, nibbling on a large chocolate-chip cookie. "I can't believe what crooks those cookie people are!" he complained. "They charged me four bucks for this. Can you believe it?"

"If it cost too much, why'd you buy it?" I asked.

"Oh, hi, Santa," Andy said. "I bought it because I had to have it. I mean, that smell was totally irresistible." Andy glanced around. "So where's Jake?"

"Guess," Josh said.

"In a store?" Andy guessed.

"Nope."

"Food court?"

"Nope."

Andy looked around again. "He didn't leave, did he?"

"Nope," Josh said. "He's right here."

"What do you mean?" Andy asked. "The only people right here are you, me, and San — " His words trailed off as his mouth fell open. He stared at me.

Crunk! The four-dollar chocolate-chip cookie fell out of his hands, hit the floor, and broke into a dozen pieces.

"Oh, my gosh, Jake!" Andy cried. "Not *you!*"

19

Andy studied me in amazement. "I can't believe it! It's you, Jake, but you look just like Santa Claus."

He took my beard in one hand and my hair in the other and pulled.

"Ow!" I grunted. "Cut it out! That hurts!"

Next, Andy looked around the mall. "But where's Mr. Dirksen's machine? Where's Santa in Jake's body?"

"It didn't happen that way this time," Josh said. "Jake just opened a card and went *whump!*"

"How do you know Santa did it?" Andy asked.

I explained how Santa had given me the red and green envelope and made me promise I wouldn't open it until I got to the mall.

"I think he wants me to see what it's like to be him," I said.

"Way cool!" Andy cried. "Now that you're Santa, you can give us everything we want!"

I felt someone tug at my sleeve. A little boy

69

with blond hair was staring up at me with big round eyes. He was wearing a blue New York Mets baseball jacket.

"Are you Santa Claus?" he asked.

"No." I shook my head.

The corners of the little boy's mouth turned down and his eyes got all squinty. "*Mommy!*" he cried and ran away.

Stunned, I looked back at Josh and Andy. "What'd I do?"

"I think you just ruined that kid's Christmas," Andy said.

"It's worse than that," Josh added. "I think you just ruined that little kid's *mother's* Christmas."

"What makes you say that?" I asked.

Josh pointed over my shoulder.

I swiveled around.

A woman was marching toward me. She was holding the little blond kid's hand. And she looked really, really mad.

20

The blond kid's mom stopped in front of me. She narrowed her eyes.

"Tell Billy that he didn't hear you correctly," she growled under her breath.

"Huh?" What was she talking about?

"I said, tell my son that he didn't hear you correctly," she hissed. "He *thinks* you said you're not Santa Claus. But that *can't possibly* be what you said, can it?"

"Well, yes, actually it — " Suddenly I felt a stabbing pain on the top of my foot. I couldn't see, but it felt like she was grinding the heel of her shoe down on Santa's boot.

"*Yeow!*" I cried out in agony and tried to bend over. But I couldn't reach my foot.

A hand grabbed my beard and yanked my head up. The next thing I knew, I was looking into the mother's steely eyes again.

"Let's start over," she said in a voice that seethed with threat. "*Who* are you?"

As she waited for my reply, she squeezed my beard tighter and tighter. It felt like she was pulling the whiskers out of my face.

"I'm Santa Claus!" I yelped.

The blond kid's mother relaxed her grip and looked down at her son. "Did you hear that, Billy? He *is* Santa."

Billy wiped the last of his tears from his eyes and smiled up at me. "Aren't you going to ask me what I want for Christmas, Santa?"

"Oh, uh, sure." I fumbled for words. "So what do you want for Christmas this year, Billy?"

"The New York Mets," Billy said.

I was sure I hadn't heard him correctly. "You mean, you want a mitt or a baseball?"

"No." Billy shook his head. "I want the New York Mets. *The whole team*. And I want Shea Stadium, too."

His mom's grip tightened on my beard again. I looked up at her. "Tell him you're working on it," she whispered.

I looked back down at Billy. "I'm working on it, Billy."

"Good. Let me know when you want me to sign the papers." Billy took his mom's hand. "Come on, Mom, let's go check out the Legos."

"By the way, very impressive beard," said Billy's mom as she let go of my whiskers and followed her son into a toy store.

"I think I just experienced Santa abuse," I moaned as I rubbed my throbbing jaw.

"That kid was a jerk," Andy said.

"You're telling me," I groaned, looking down at my scrunched-up beard.

"He should have asked for the Giants," Andy said. "It's a much better franchise. Better stadium, too."

"Just because Billy didn't ask for the Giants doesn't mean one of these kids won't," Josh said.

"One of what kids?" I asked.

"Take a look, *Santa*." Josh pointed.

I looked up . . . and into a sea of little kids' faces.

"Santa! Santa!" They all started to scream and reach toward me.

Dozens of little hands were grabbing at my bright red Santa suit.

"Goo-goo, gah-gah." Drooling babies in their parents' arms were pulling at my hair and beard.

Everyone was crowding in around Josh, Andy, and me.

Oh, no! *I was trapped in Santa's body!*

21

A ndy, Josh, and I stood with our backs to each other as we faced the growing crowd pressing in all on all sides.

"What are we going to do?" I asked.

"We're gonna get out of here," Andy said. "And then, since you're Santa, you can give us everything we want."

"I'm not going to do that," I said.

"Why not?" Andy asked.

"Because it's not right."

"Are you crazy?" Andy said. "This is the chance of a lifetime! Forget the toys. You can set us up in mansions with racing cars and private helicopters."

"No." I shook my head.

"Why not?" Andy asked. "We're your friends. Right, Josh?"

Josh pressed his lips together solemnly. "I hate to say this, Andy, but I agree with Jake. I don't

74

think he should give us everything we want, even if he *is* Santa."

Andy stared at us in disbelief. Meanwhile, the crowd kept pressing in toward us. Everyone was pushing and shoving. They were reaching toward me and calling out for Santa.

"I'd still like to know what we're going to do," I said as we were jostled this way and that.

"What's this *we* stuff?" Andy sputtered. "*You're* the one who had to turn into Santa Claus. I just came to the mall to get some fax paper. Excuse me, folks!" He started to push his way out of the crowd.

"Traitor!" I shouted after him. Then I turned to Josh. "You're not going to desert me, too, are you?"

"I don't know why not," Josh grunted as we were squeezed by the crowd. "It's not me they want. It's you."

"But you can't just leave me," I begged him. "I thought we were friends."

"We are friends," Josh said. "But what am I supposed to do?"

"You're supposed to tell me what I'm supposed to do," I said.

The mob of kids around us had stopped chanting Santa's name. Now they were shouting out what they wanted for Christmas.

"Santa! I want a game system!"

"I want a computer!"

"I want a bike!"

"A horse!"

"A dollhouse!"

"A swimming pool!"

"I think you better start giving them stuff," Josh suggested. "It's the only way you'll get rid of them."

"But how do I know they'll really get what I promise them?" I asked. "I'm not really Santa."

"Maybe not," Josh said. "But they *think* you're Santa, and that's the only thing that matters."

I didn't know if he was right or not. But I did know that if I didn't do something fast, we were going to get trampled. So I looked down at a boy with red hair, freckles, and glasses. "What did you say you wanted?"

"I want a swimming pool," the kid said.

"You got it," I said.

"Oh, wow!" the kid shouted with glee. "Wait till I tell my dad!"

The red-haired kid started to work his way out of the crowd. He was immediately replaced by a girl with short curly black hair.

"And what do you want?" I asked.

"Straight hair," she said.

"It's all yours," I said.

Her mouth fell open and her eyes went wide. "Oh, thank you so much, Santa!"

She was replaced by another kid.

And another.

And another.

No matter what they asked for, I told them they could have it. Baby brothers, motorcycles, small South American countries — I promised them everything and anything.

The funny thing was, you never saw a happier bunch of kids.

"I don't see what's so bad about this," I said to Josh after a while. "It seems like I'm making an awful lot of kids happy, doesn't it?"

"You may be making kids happy," Josh replied, "but I don't think you're doing such a hot job with their parents."

No sooner were the words out of his mouth than a man with red hair, freckles, and glasses appeared before me. He looked very annoyed. With him was a familiar-looking kid who also had red hair, freckles, and glasses.

"Did you tell my son he was going to get a swimming pool for Christmas?" the man asked.

"Uh . . . yes, I guess I did," I replied nervously.

"And who's going to pay for it?" the man asked angrily.

I didn't know what to say. Next a woman with short curly black hair came up to me.

"You promised my daughter straight hair?" she asked.

"Well, I . . . "

"What am I going to tell her on Christmas

morning when she wakes up and still has curly hair?" the woman demanded.

Other angry parents began to show up.

"How am I supposed to give my daughter a baby brother?"

"Where am I going to get a South American country?"

They were all really peeved.

Things were starting to look bad.

22

"**E**xcuse me!" a voice yelled. "Watch out! Coming through!"

A skinny man with black hair and a thin black mustache pushed toward me through the crowd. Andy was following him. The kids around me weren't happy as the skinny man pushed them aside.

"Hey, where do you think you're going?" one of them yelled.

"Get in line!" shouted another kid.

"You have to wait your turn like we did!"

"Sorry, kids, but this is business," the man replied. He finally got close enough to offer me his hand. I shook it.

"Hello, Santa, glad you could make it," he said.

"Thanks, but who are you?" I asked.

"Stanley Greedlick," the man said. "I own Maximum Pro-Fit Sports."

He pointed at a huge store filled with awesome gear and sports clothes. Inside were aisles and aisles of basketball shoes and soccer and baseball cleats. There were floor to ceiling displays of tennis rackets, baseball mitts, basketball hoops, football uniforms, punching bags, and fishing rods.

It was every teenaged guy's idea of Heaven.

"You *own* that store?" I was dumbfounded.

"Believe it, Santa," he said. "Now listen, you can't stand out here in the middle of the mall like this. It's dangerous. You're getting mobbed."

"You're not going to make Santa leave, are you?" cried a kid standing near us.

"No, I'd never do that," Mr. Greedlick replied. "I just want to provide him with some organization and crowd control. The kind of protection a celebrity like Santa deserves. What do you say, Santa?"

At that moment, protection, organization, and crowd control sounded really good. And I didn't mind being called a celebrity, either.

"I like it," I said.

"Then come this way." Stanley Greedlick started to lead Josh and me through the crowd.

"Hey, wait!" the kids started to scream.

"Where's Santa going?"

"He hasn't heard what I want yet!"

"Don't worry, everyone," Stanley Greedlick yelled back. "Santa's just going over to my store. You can all come and visit him there."

We headed toward Maximum Pro-Fit Sports,

and the crowd of kids and parents quickly followed. Inside Josh and I stopped and looked around. Parked near us was a whole rack of Fat Wheels mountain bikes.

"Oh, wow!" I said in awe. "I can't believe they have them."

"I can believe it," Josh whispered back, showing me the price tag. "See what they're charging?"

I felt my eyes bulge out. "Gosh, you could almost buy a used car for that much!"

"Back this way, Santa." Stanley Greedlick pointed toward the back of the store.

"Wait," I said. "Shouldn't I be near the front where people can see me?"

"Absolutely not," Mr. Greedlick said in a low voice. "I want you in the *back* of the store. That way the people have to pass all my goods to get to you. The whole idea is to get them interested in buying Maximum Pro-Fit sports equipment."

"I thought the whole idea was to let them meet Santa," I said.

"You bet." Mr. Greedlick winked.

At the back of the store, Mr. Greedlick's salespeople had set up a chair for me. As the crowd of parents and kids followed us, the Maximum Pro-Fit salespeople made them get in a long line. Next to the line, they set up TV monitors with VCRs.

"It's really nice of you to set up the VCRs so the little kids have something to watch while they wait on line," I said.

"Thanks," said Mr. Greedlick. "I always think of the customer. That's the key to my success."

"Now that you're being taken care of, Jake, I mean, Santa," Josh said, "I'm going to get myself some lunch." He headed off toward the food court.

I sat down in the chair. A little girl with brown hair came up to me, followed by her father. The girl sat in my lap.

"So what would you like for Christmas?" I asked.

"I want a stable for my toy horses," she said.

Before answering, I looked up at her father. By now I'd figured out that I couldn't promise something without checking with the parents first. The little girl's father nodded.

"I think that's a very nice thing to ask for," I told the girl. "And I bet when you look under the tree on Christmas morning you'll find it."

"Oh, thank you, Santa!" the girl gushed. "Thank you so much!"

She slid off my lap, and a little boy wearing a toy Army helmet climbed on. "And what would you like for Christmas?" I asked.

"A machine gun," the boy said.

I looked up at his mother. She shook her head and mouthed, "No guns."

I turned back to the boy. "I'm afraid I don't have any guns this Christmas."

"How about a bazooka?" the kid asked.

"We've run out of them," I said.

"A hand grenade?" the kid said hopefully.

I shook my head.

The kid scrunched up his forehead. "Then what can I get?"

"Maybe he'd like a Maxi Pro-Fit four-wheel drive turbo skateboard," whispered Mr. Greedlick, who was standing behind me.

"Shouldn't we let the kid decide for himself?" I whispered back.

"No, that's not part of the deal," said Mr. Greedlick.

"What deal?" I asked.

"The deal your friend made."

"I don't know what you're talking about," I said.

"I'll be right back." Mr. Greedlick left.

23

The next kid on my lap was a little girl who wanted a Maximum Pro-Fit inflatable dinghy with a three-horsepower outboard motor.

"How did you get the idea for that?" I asked.

The girl pointed at one of the TV monitors Mr. Greedlick had set up next to the line of people waiting to see me. "I saw it on the TV."

"I thought those TVs were showing movies or something," I said.

"No way," said the little girl. "It shows all the things you can buy here in the store."

It figures, I thought. Mr. Greedlick's way of entertaining kids was showing them nonstop advertisements. Now Andy showed up at my side.

"Listen," he whispered in my ear. "When a kid says he doesn't know what he wants, you're supposed to suggest something his parents can buy here at Maximum Pro-Fit Sports."

"Why?" I asked.

"Because that's the deal I made," he said.

"What deal?" I asked.

"The deal for a discount on a Fat Wheels mountain bike," Andy said.

I could hardly believe my ears. "You arranged to get me a discount on a Fat Wheels? Gee, Andy, that's really nice."

Andy cleared his throat awkwardly. "Well, actually, the bike's for me, not you."

24

"What?" I thought I must have heard him wrong.

"*You* wouldn't give me anything, so I figured out a way to get something myself," Andy explained.

"Well, forget it," I said. "There's no way I'm going to sit here in this Santa suit and listen to all these kids just so you can get a good deal on a Fat Wheels mountain bike."

I started to get up, but the crowd instantly began to shout protests.

"Wait, Santa! Where are you going?"

"You just got here!"

"Stop, Santa! You can't leave!"

Seeing all their pleading, unhappy faces made me decide to sit down again. As soon as I did, another little kid climbed into my lap and asked for a present.

* * *

The afternoon passed slowly. Josh came back from lunch and said he would get Santa the fax paper. At the back of the crowd I saw Andy shaking hands with Mr. Greedlick. They were both smiling, as if their deal was a success. Judging from how crowded Maximum Pro-Fit Sports was, it sure looked like a success to me.

Meanwhile, kid after kid climbed into my lap and asked for present after present.

The Santa suit was hot. My face felt flushed and my throat was dry and sore from talking.

The line of kids and their parents looked endless.

I began to understand why Santa felt like quitting. Who in the world would *want* a job like this?

A little blond boy had just crawled off my lap. I'd already forgotten what he'd asked for. A little girl with brown pigtails crawled on next.

"And what would you like for Christmas?" I asked automatically. I hardly even heard what they said anymore. Instead I'd just glance around for someone who looked like a parent. If the parent nodded, I told the kids they could have whatever they'd asked for. If the parent shook his head, I told the kids it was out of stock.

This time I didn't hear anything. I was so tired and miserable, I assumed I must have missed her request completely. Once again I said, "And what would you like for Christmas?"

"Just look, Santa," the little girl said.

I looked down. She was holding up a paper cup of water.

"What's this for?" I asked.

"It's for you," she said.

"Why?" I asked.

"Because you look hot and tired," she said.

I blinked. "You . . . brought this for me?"

"That's okay, isn't it?" she asked.

"Why, yes, it's totally okay." I couldn't believe it! Someone had actually brought *me* a gift.

"Go ahead," she said, holding the cup higher. "Have some."

I gratefully took the cup from her and sipped the cool, refreshing water. My throat felt one hundred times better! And it was only a cup of water. It wasn't even some fancy sport ade drink loaded with protein and minerals and hydrolites.

But it was all I wanted.

I finished the cup. "That was great."

The little girl smiled up at me. "Want some more, Santa?"

"No, thanks, that was all I needed," I said. I wasn't sure what felt better — the water, or knowing that someone was thoughtful enough to bring it to me.

"So what's your name?" I asked.

"Rainy," she said.

"Rainy?" I repeated. "I've never heard a name like that."

"It's short for Lorraine," she explained.

"So tell me, Rainy," I said, "what would you like for Christmas?"

Rainy just shrugged.

"Oh, come on," I said. "There must be *something* you want."

"I want a dollhouse, but I already know I'm going to get it because my dad said so," she replied.

"Couldn't I get it for you?" I asked.

"You don't have to," Rainy said. "I know my dad will do it. You can help other kids instead."

"Then why did you wait on line to see me?" I asked.

"To give you the water," she said.

I couldn't believe it. This little girl on my lap almost brought tears to my eyes. I was so grateful to her for bringing me the water. And for *not* wanting anything in return. I would have given her anything she'd asked for.

Even if I had to pay for it myself.

"Hey, come on, Santa, let's get going," grunted a man in line with a little boy.

"Yeah, Santa," muttered a mother. "We don't have all day, you know."

"Get on the ball, Santa," a voice whispered in my ear. "You have to keep the line moving."

I looked up into the face of Stanley Greedlick.

"You know how the game works," he whispered. "You have to keep the customers happy."

I looked back down at Rainy. "I guess you have to go."

89

"It's okay, Santa." She smiled back at me, then slid off my lap. As she walked away, she turned and waved.

It was nice to know that there were kids like her around.

25

I stayed until the lights in Maximum Pro-Fit Sports began to dim. An announcement over the loudspeaker said that the store was closing. The last little kid sat on my lap and asked for a game system, and then there was no one else on line.

"Great job, Santa." Stanley Greedlick patted me on the shoulder. "I bet we did more business today than any other store in the mall, thanks to you."

He handed me a slip of white paper with some writing on it. "And just to show you how much I appreciate your hard work, here's a Maximum Pro-Fit ten-dollar gift certificate good any time."

"Gee, thanks," I said.

"So what time will you be back tomorrow?" he asked.

"I'm afraid I can't come back tomorrow," I said, trying to be polite. "I have school."

"School?" Stanley Greedlick grinned. "That's a

good one, Santa. But seriously, could you be here when the store opens?"

"No." I shook my head.

"Oh, now I understand," he said. "You're playing hard to get. You want something in return. Okay, Santa, what will it take to get you to come back?"

I didn't understand. "What do you mean?"

"I mean, what do you want in return?" he asked. "I know you don't do this for free. Today I gave your friend a good deal on that Fat Wheels mountain bike. Perhaps tomorrow you'd like something for yourself."

Maybe I was just too tired to think. Or I was in a strange mood. But at that moment I didn't want anything. All I wanted to do was go home and sleep.

"I'm sorry," I said. "There's nothing I want."

"Hey, come on, everybody wants something," Stanley Greedlick said.

"Listen, Mr. Greedlick," I said. "You had a great day today and did a ton of business. You should be thankful."

I started to walk toward the front of the store. Stanley Greedlick quickly followed.

"Don't get me wrong, Santa," he said. "Of course I'm thankful. But why stop? Just think how much business we could do between now and Christmas."

I gave him a look. "How much business *we*

could do? I think you mean how much business *you* could do."

"That's why I want to know what you want," Stanley Greedlick said. "You name it, Santa. You want a Fat Wheels mountain bike for *free*? Just say the word and it's yours."

I didn't say the word. Instead, I left the store and started to walk through the mall. It was almost empty now. The only people left were the cleaning crew, sweeping up empty cups and candy wrappers.

"Hey, come on, Santa, you can't just walk out on me." Stanley Greedlick was starting to sound desperate.

"I'm sorry, but I can't come back tomorrow," I said. I really did have school, even if he didn't believe me.

"You *have* to!" Mr. Greedlick insisted. "How can you do this to me? With you here I could make a fortune!"

"No," I said firmly.

Stanley Greedlick stopped and grit his teeth angrily. "And you have the nerve to call yourself Santa Claus?" he shouted, shaking his fist at me. "Don't you know you're supposed to give? If it wasn't for you, I'd be rich! You're nothing but a no-good bum!"

26

"*Nothing but a no-good bum . . .* " The words echoed in my head. No wonder Santa Claus was ready to quit. Everyone wanted him to give until they got what they wanted. And if he stopped, he was a bum.

I left the mall. It was dark and cold outside, and I was beyond tired. All around me, people were getting into their cars and driving out of the parking lot. Some cars were filled with so many presents the drivers couldn't even see out the back windows. In other cars babies were crying and kids were screaming and fighting. In a few cars the kids pressed their faces against the windows and stared at me silently, as if they couldn't believe Santa had to walk.

"Yo, Santa!" someone called. I turned and saw some teenagers in a car. One of them rolled down the window and waved. He had a shaved head and was wearing earrings in both ears.

I waved back.

"Know what, Santa?" he shouted. "You're so fat you need directions to find your belly button!"

Now another kid stuck his shaved head out. "You're so fat, your blood type is Ragú!"

The car erupted with laughter. I couldn't believe it! Even Santa got dissed!

As the car went past, a guy in the backseat pointed his finger at me in a menacing way. Like the others, his head was shaved nearly bald, and earrings hung from both of his ears. But he looked younger.

And sort of familiar.

Then I realized, *it was Barry Dunn*!

I felt my jaw drop with surprise, but then I smiled. Barry didn't know it, but I'd already gotten him back. He wasn't getting anything from Santa this Christmas.

In the back of the car, Barry saw me smile. His eyes narrowed until they were thin slits.

Screech! With its tires smoking, the car left rubber out of the parking lot.

Good riddance, I thought.

I trudged along the road toward home. Those stiff leather Santa boots felt heavy on my feet. It was dark and lonely. The only light came from the headlights of passing cars. Some had Christmas trees tied to the roof or in the trunk. Some were filled with kids or presents. Hardly any of them noticed Santa Claus shuffling along by himself.

So this was how the real Santa must have felt.

The world was passing him by.

Everyone was in too much of a rush.

Everyone was too busy asking for stuff to think of stopping and offering him a ride.

Then I sensed a car behind me.

I turned to look, but the headlights were blinding.

The car was slowing down. I felt relieved. Someone had finally noticed Santa and was slowing down to see if he needed a lift.

The car pulled up beside me and stopped. The window went down.

I expected to see a friendly face.

But the face that looked out at me wasn't friendly.

It was Barry Dunn.

27

"What's so funny, Santa?" Barry growled.

"Did I say something was funny?" I asked back.

"You smiled at me," Barry said.

"So?"

Barry glowered at me. I knew he was trying to act tough and show off for the older guys in the car.

"You're not allowed to smile at me unless I give you permission," Barry said. "Say you're sorry."

I probably should have said I was sorry and then forgotten about it. But I was tired and irritable. Santa didn't deserve to be treated this way.

"Say you're sorry," Barry repeated, "or I'll give you a Christmas present you'll never forget."

Instead of saying I was sorry, I said, "Barry, you are so dumb if your brain was dynamite, you wouldn't have enough to blow your nose."

Barry's mouth fell open in surprise.

I wasn't finished. "You're so lame you called the

operator and asked for the number of 911. You're so thick you need a recipe to make ice cubes. And you're so dim you stayed up all night studying for your blood test."

Barry was speechless. The other guys in the car began to snicker. I really should have shut my mouth, but all those pent-up frustrations just poured out of me.

"You're so stupid you tried to wake up a sleeping bag," I went on. "You're so wacked you broke into a house and couldn't get out. And finally, you're so mental you fell out of the family tree and they wouldn't let you back in."

The older guys in the car started to laugh. Barry's face turned red. He was grinding his teeth so hard it sounded like coarse sandpaper.

"You gonna let Santa cut you down like that?" one of the older guys asked him.

"No way!" Barry pushed open the car door and jumped out.

The next thing I knew, I was running for my life.

28

It wasn't easy to run in those big Santa boots and with that big Santa belly. But at least I didn't have a big Santa butt. And now I understood why Santa put his hair in a ponytail to keep it out of his eyes. Every time I turned my head to see if Barry was gaining on me, I got a face full of white hair.

Barry was definitely gaining on me.

And he was being followed by the older guys who'd been in the car with him.

"Go get him, Barry!" one of them shouted gleefully.

"You'll show Santa who's the boss!" laughed another.

I could hear Barry's footsteps slapping against the pavement as he got closer. He was breathing hard. "I'm gonna get you, Santa!"

"Don't you believe in me?" I yelled back as I ran ahead of him.

"I believe you're gonna be so black-and-blue

that even your own reindeer won't recognize you," he shouted.

I had just reached a corner when I felt his hand clamp down on my shoulder. I turned right. Luckily, Barry slipped on some sand and lost his grip.

I ran down a street lined with houses. Up ahead I saw a brightly lit house decorated with colorful lights and big plastic candy canes and snowmen. A man had just gotten out of his car and was walking toward the front door. I ran up to him.

"Excuse me, sir!" I cried, breathing hard.

The man frowned. "What do you want?"

"I'm being chased." I pointed back at Barry and his buddies. "Could I just come inside and wait until they go away?"

The man looked down the street at Barry and his friends, and then back at me. He shook his head. "Sorry."

"But I need help," I begged.

"Call your elves." The man went into his house and slammed the door.

I started to run again, but I was getting tired. Barry and his friends were getting closer. I ran past a few more houses and then turned up a dark driveway. Maybe I'd get lucky. Maybe I could hide. Or maybe someone would be there to help me.

I got to the garage door at the end of the driveway and tried to open it.

It was locked!

I heard footsteps behind me and turned. Barry and his buddies were at the bottom of the driveway.

Too tired to run anymore, I pressed my back against the garage door.

Barry started up the driveway toward me. He slipped off his jacket and started to roll up his sleeves.

"What's wrong, Santa?" he asked with a nasty-looking smirk on his lips. "Run out of believers?"

29

"You should believe in me," I said, still panting for breath.

"Why's that?" Barry asked. By now his friends had caught up to us and were standing behind him.

"Because I'm real," I said.

"Yeah, right," Barry chuckled. "If you're real, what am I getting for Christmas?"

"Nothing," I said. "Because as usual, you've been naughty."

Barry made a fist and stepped toward me. "Then I guess I have nothing to lose by beating you into a pulp."

I realized I'd just made a mistake. "On second thought," I quickly added, "maybe we can make a deal. If you let me go, I'll see if I can get you something."

"Forget it, Santa," Barry snarled. "I already know what I want for Christmas — your head on a platter."

"Get him, Barry," one of the older guys urged him.

Barry took another step toward me. My back was pressed against the garage door. Barry's buddies spread out to my right and left to make sure I couldn't escape.

In desperation, I shut my eyes and prayed: *Santa, if you can hear me . . . what should I do?*

To my total surprise, a voice in my head answered: *Use karate.*

I couldn't believe it! *Santa knows karate?* I thought.

Hey, the voice answered, *that's a black belt you're wearing, isn't it?*

I looked down at Santa's wide black belt. *Are you serious?*

Well, no, actually, the voice answered. *I signed up for the classes, but I never got around to going.*

Barry Dunn cracked his knuckles and took another step toward me.

This is no time for jokes, Santa! I thought desperately.

Okay, okay, here's what you do, the voice said. I listened carefully, then looked up at Barry.

"All right, Barry," I said. "This is your last chance. Back off now and you'll get that amateur magic kit you've been secretly wishing for."

"Hey, did you hear that?" one of the older guys laughed. "Santa says Barry wants an amateur magic kit!"

"Aw, isn't that cute?" chortled another. "Santa thinks Barry wants to learn card tricks."

But Barry scowled and leaned close to me. "How'd you know about that?" he asked in a low voice.

"Because I'm Santa," I whispered back.

Barry's forehead wrinkled and he glanced at his friends out of the corners of his eyes.

"Go on, Barry," one of them said. "Why don't you show Santa some magic . . . with your fists."

Barry raised his fists.

"You want to see some *real* magic, Barry?" I asked.

Barry hesitated and gave me a suspicious look.

"Do you think your friends are men, or mice?" I asked.

"Men," Barry answered.

"Think again," I said.

30

Phooomm! A sudden cloud of smoke enveloped Barry's friends. When it cleared, they were gone. All that remained were their boots on the driveway.

Barry looked around and blinked. "Where'd they go?"

"They're still here," I said.

"Where?" Barry asked.

"Check out the boots."

Barry kneeled down and peered into one of the boots. A little mouse poked his nose out.

"*Ahhh!*" Barry screamed and jumped to his feet. He stared at me with wide eyes. "How'd you do that?"

"Easy," I said with a smile. "When you're Santa, stuff happens."

Barry started to back away. "You're not gonna turn me into a mouse, are you?"

"I will if you don't stop being naughty," I said.

"Hey, I promise," Barry said with a quavering

voice. "I'll never be naughty again."

"From now on you're going to be nice, right?" I said.

"Right," Barry agreed eagerly.

"No more picking on kids," I said.

"Right," Barry agreed.

"No more dissing Santa Claus."

"Definitely. I promise."

"Okay, get out of here," I said.

Barry looked surprised. "You mean, I can just go?"

"That's right," I said. "But don't forget, from now on no more Mr. Naughty Guy."

"Believe it." Barry Dunn turned and ran away into the dark.

I heaved a weary sigh and looked down at the boots in the driveway. The mice were still peeking out of them, twitching their little noses. Santa had said they'd turn back into humans in a few minutes.

Too bad.

I started to walk home again. It was even darker now, and later. And my feet hurt after all that running. I got back to the main road and headed toward my house. But it had been a really long day and I hadn't gotten much sleep the night before. I was totally wiped out.

I came to a bench along the side of the road and sat down to rest. What a day . . . Who would have believed that Santa really existed and could do all the stuff he'd done?

I looked down at the Santa boots. Inside them my tired feet ached. The day before I'd had a list of fifteen things I'd wanted for Christmas. But now I would have traded them all for a simple ride home.

Just then a city bus pulled up to the curb and stopped.

The doors opened.

I looked around and realized that the bench I was sitting on was part of a bus stop.

"You coming?" the driver asked.

I searched all of Santa's pockets, but they were empty.

"I . . . I don't have any money," I said.

A smile appeared on the bus driver's face. "Hop on anyway. Since when does Santa need bus fare?"

31

I'm not sure I would have made it home without
the ride from that friendly bus driver. As I
trudged up my driveway, I noticed a pickup truck
parked at the curb. The sides of the pickup were
covered with a thin film of dirt, as if it had been
traveling for a long time.

The lights were off in my house. My parents
and sister weren't back yet from Aunt Elma's.

I let myself in the front door.

Whump!

The change back to Jake caught me by surprise. I touched my face and head. The beard and
long hair were gone. I looked down. The big belly
was gone. I could see my feet again.

"Santa?" I called.

No one answered.

Was he gone? Oh, no! I didn't want him to leave
yet. There was stuff I had to tell him.

I thought of the cloud-runner and ran out to the
backyard. I was in luck! Santa was still there. He

was watching a couple of kids in green coveralls work on the cloud-runner.

But when I got closer, I noticed that those "kids" had pointy ears.

They weren't kids at all! They were elves!

They'd lifted the seat off the cloud-runner and were working on the engine inside.

They weren't just elves! They were elf mechanics!

I walked up behind Santa and was just about to say hello when he turned as if he knew I was there.

"So, how did you like being Santa?" he asked.

"I can see why you'd want to quit," I admitted. "It's not a lot of fun being you these days."

Santa nodded. "Can you blame me?"

"But what about the people who still believe in giving?" I asked. "If you quit it won't be fair to them."

"I know." Santa sighed wistfully. "That's what makes it such a hard decision. Believe me, Jake, I've tried. I've been trying for a long time. But it just gets harder and harder. Everyone deserves a rest, even Santa Claus."

I couldn't argue with that. I'd only been Santa for a day and I was exhausted. Doing it for fifteen hundred years must have been a total wipeout!

One of the elf mechanics looked up from the cloud-runner. "I hate to say this, Santa, but this thing's wrecked."

"I never should have let those animal rights people talk me out of using Rudolph and the other reindeer," Santa moped.

I yawned and felt more tired than ever. My eyelids and arms felt heavy. I couldn't remember being so exhausted.

"Looks like you ought to go to bed, Jake," Santa said. "And don't worry about the cloud-runner. We'll have it out of your backyard by the morning."

"No sweat, Santa." I started back toward the house. But then I thought of something and stopped. "Santa?"

He looked up from the cloud-runner. "Yes?"

"Thanks for helping me with Barry Dunn and his friends."

"No problem," Santa said.

"And there's just one thing I wanted to ask for before you quit," I said.

The furrows in Santa's broad forehead deepened and he didn't look happy. He was probably wondering how, after all I'd been through that day, I could still be thinking of asking for something.

"What's that, Jake?" he asked warily.

"There are these two people," I said. "One's a little girl named Rainy and the other's a city bus driver. I just wanted to ask you not to forget them."

"Don't worry, Jake, I won't."

110

"Thanks, Santa." I turned and headed toward the house.

"But, Jake," Santa called behind me.

I stopped. "Yeah?"

"It was nice of you to think of them."

I was about to say good night when I thought of something else. "One last question?"

"Go ahead," Santa said.

"You know your big white mustache?" I said. "When you blow your nose, how do you keep the boogers from getting into it?"

"That," Santa replied, "is my business."

We shared a smile.

"G'night, Santa," I said.

"G'night, Jake, and merry Christmas."

32

*D**ing dong!*
The sound of the doorbell woke me the next morning. I opened my eyes and looked at the clock. Nine A.M.? Oh, no! I was late for school!

Ding dong! The bell rang again. Why didn't anyone in my family answer it? Where were they anyway? How come Mom hadn't gotten me up for school the way she usually did?

Ding dong!

I pulled on my robe and left my room.

Groof! Lance met me in the hall, wagging his tail.

"What are you doing here?" I asked. "Why didn't they feed you and let you out in the back?"

Then I noticed that not a single light in the house was on. It felt very quiet and empty.

"Hello?" I called out. "Anyone here?"

No one answered. It didn't make sense. Mom, Dad, and Jessica should have come home last night from Aunt Elma's. Like me, Jessica had school today. And Mom and Dad both had work.

Ding dong!

"Who is it?" I called as I went toward the front door.

"Josh and Andy, who do you think?" Josh called back.

Huh? I pulled open the door.

"What are you guys doing here?" I asked.

"What are you talking about, Jake?" Josh said. "We have big plans for today, remember? We're going to watch movies and play video games and eat junk food all day."

"No, that was yesterday," I said.

Josh and Andy both looked puzzled.

"Yesterday?" Andy said. "Your parents were around yesterday. Today's the day they're off visiting your aunt whoever-she-is. We've got the house all to ourselves."

Wait a minute. None of this made any sense unless . . . "What day is today?"

"Sunday," Josh and Andy both answered.

"You sure it isn't Monday?" I asked.

"If it was Monday, we'd be in school," Josh said.

"Unfortunately," Andy added.

"You don't remember going to the mall yesterday?" I asked. "You don't remember me turning into Santa Claus? You don't remember us getting mobbed or Andy making a deal with the owner of Maximum Pro-Fit Sports to get a Fat Wheels mountain bike?"

Josh reached forward and pressed his hand against my forehead. "Are you feeling okay, Jake?"

"Just swear to me that you don't remember any of that," I said.

Both Josh and Andy swore.

Was it possible that it was all a dream?

"Excuse me, guys." I went past them and outside.

"Where are you going?" Andy asked.

"You know you're only wearing your pajamas and a robe," Josh reminded me.

"I know," I said as I headed around to the backyard.

The cloud-runner was gone.

"What's going on?" Andy asked as he and Josh caught up to me. "Why are we in the backyard?"

"I'm not sure," I said.

How could it have been a dream?

The cold breeze blew and made me shiver. I pulled my robe tight and slid my hands into the pockets. I felt something in one of the pockets and pulled it out.

It was the red and green envelope!

"Someone sent you a Christmas card?" Andy guessed.

I shook my head. The envelope was sealed. I tore it open.

Inside was a blue bus ticket. The destination said: Heartland.

"You going somewhere?" Josh asked.

I put the ticket in my pocket. "You better believe it."

33

Heartland isn't much of a town. Just a main street with some stores, a bank, a post office, and a library. No malls, no fast food, no arcades. The movie house is open on Wednesdays, Fridays, and Saturdays, and it only shows one movie at a time.

They don't even have cable.

I got off the bus and walked to Aunt Elma's house. The scent of burning wood was in the air, and a bunch of people were skating on a frozen pond nearby.

Aunt Elma's house was small and white. A wreath hung on the front door. I went up the steps and knocked.

Jessica answered it and instantly looked shocked. "Jake! What are you doing here?"

"I changed my mind," I said.

She stared at me in wonder, focusing on the bright red scarf around my neck. "Why are you wearing *that*?"

"Guess," I said.

Now Mom and Dad joined her at the door. They both looked equally as stunned.

"How did you get here?" Mom asked.

"The bus," I said.

"Who is it? Who's there?" an older woman's voice asked. Mom and Dad parted to make room for Aunt Elma. When my white-haired aunt saw me, her face lit up. "Oh, Jake, sweetheart! I knew you'd come! And you're just in time for dinner."

She took my face in her hands and gave me a big kiss on the cheek. "Now come in and get out of the cold."

I stepped into the house. It smelled like fresh-baked bread and cookies.

"I'm so glad you're wearing the scarf I made you last year," Aunt Elma said. "And guess what?"

"What?" I asked.

"This year I made you a bright red hat and mittens to match."

"That's great," I said. "Thanks."

Over Aunt Elma's shoulder, I saw my parents and sister giving me skeptical looks. My aunt hugged me.

"Oh, I'm so happy you're here!" She sounded truly delighted. "Just let me go back into the kitchen and finish cooking. Then we'll all eat."

Aunt Elma went into the kitchen. The rest of the family stayed behind.

"I can't begin to tell you how happy you've made her," Mom said. "Thank you for coming, Jake."

"You made the right decision, Jake," Dad said with a wink. "The cookies are better than ever this year."

Mom and Dad went into the dining room. Jessica stayed behind and stepped close to me. She peered into my eyes like a doctor would. "Is that really Jake in there? Or did you switch bodies with someone?"

"It's really me," I said.

"Are you sure?" she asked suspiciously.

"Yes."

"Then there has to be something more to this," she said. "There's something you haven't told me."

"You're right," I said.

"You didn't burn down the house!" she gasped.

"Nope," I said. "Everything's fine."

"You broke something of mine?"

"No."

"You got into some kind of trouble?" my sister guessed next.

I shook my head.

"Then I don't get it," she said. "What are you doing here, Jake?"

"Just getting into the spirit of Christmas," I said with a smile.

34

The dinner Aunt Elma made was really good, and Dad was right about the cookies. They were the best. Afterward everyone exchanged presents. I gave Aunt Elma a small white box with a red bow. We all watched as she opened it.

"A hockey puck!" she cried happily. "Oh, Jake, that's so sweet of you!"

"I wasn't sure if you were still playing hockey or not," I said.

"I don't play much anymore," Aunt Elma said. "But it will make a great paperweight."

Then, just like Aunt Elma promised, I got the red knit cap and gloves to match my scarf.

We helped clean up the dinner dishes, and then it was time to go. Aunt Elma stood in the doorway and watched as we got into the car. Dad backed out of the driveway and we all gave her one last wave and settled in for the long drive home.

Mom looked over the front seat at me. She was

smiling. "I can't thank you enough for coming, Jake. You made Aunt Elma very, very happy."

"It was the least I could do," I said.

Mom turned around. Now the only one staring at me was Jessica, sitting next to me in the backseat. "I can't believe you gave Aunt Elma a hockey puck," she whispered.

"Hey, it's the thought that counts," I said. I didn't want to tell her that the puck was about the only thing I could afford with my Maximum Pro-Fit Sports gift certificate.

We got onto the highway and headed back toward Jeffersonville. I gazed out the window, knowing I'd done the right thing and feeling good about it.

Dad pulled into the left lane to pass a pickup truck ahead of us. As we caught up to it, I noticed a red and green wave-runner in the back.

At first I thought that was a pretty funny coincidence. Then I saw the thin film of dirt on the pickup's sides. Someone had rubbed a message in the dirt with his finger. It read:

NORTH POLE OR BUST

As we passed the pickup, I looked up at the driver. He was wearing yellow aviator glasses and a brown leather bomber jacket. He had red cheeks. His long white hair was pulled back into a ponytail.

His long white beard was pulled into a ponytail, too.

Sitting in the truck next to him were two short guys with hats pulled low over their ears.

North Pole or bust?

What about Las Vegas?

As I stared up at the driver in disbelief, he looked down at me and gave me a thumbs-up.

Suddenly I felt something in my shirt pocket. I reached in and pulled out another red and green envelope.

I tore it open. Inside was a card. The message was written in the large looping letters I recognized as Santa's handwriting.

It said:

YOU HELPED ME CHANGE MY MIND, JAKE.
MERRY CHRISTMAS — SANTA

Todd Strasser has written many award-winning novels for young and teenage readers. Among his best-known books are *Help! I'm Trapped in Obedience School* and *Girl Gives Birth to Own Prom Date*. His most recent project for Scholastic was *Camp Run-a-Muck*, a series about a summer camp where anything can happen.

Todd speaks frequently at schools about the craft of writing and conducts writing workshops for young people. He and his family live outside New York City with their yellow Labrador retriever, Mac.

Like Santa, Todd has a beard, but it hasn't turned all white . . . yet.